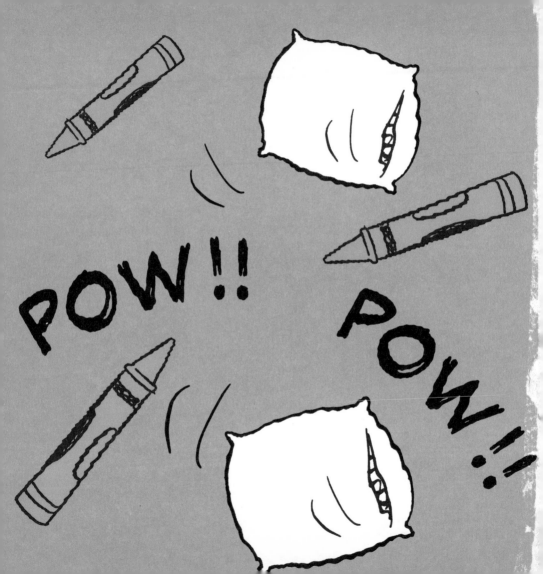

Siblings
(Should Never Be In The Same Family!)

by
SCHULZ

HarperCollins*Publishers*

Are You Sure We're Related?

Are You Sure We're Related?

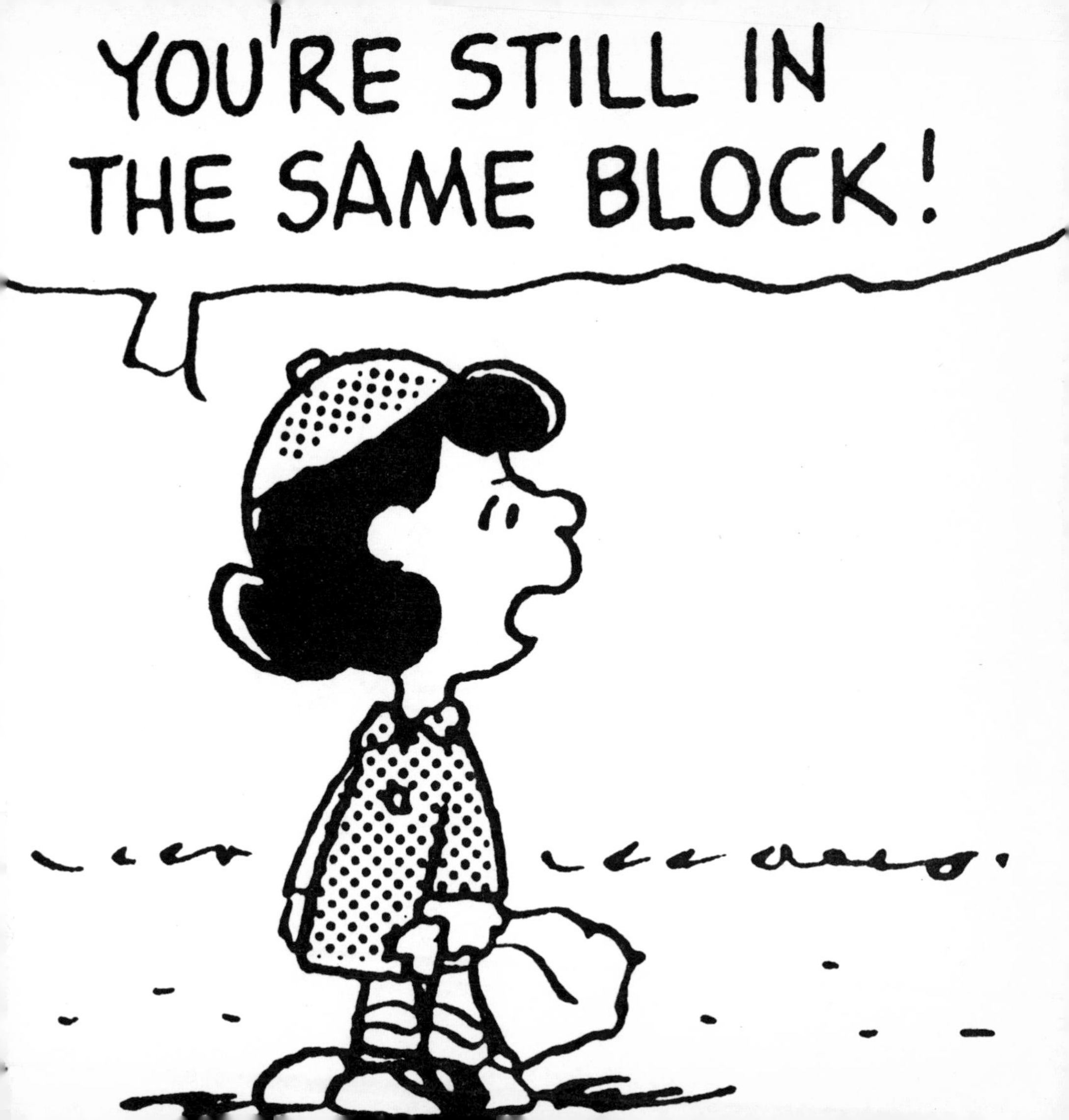
YOU'RE STILL IN THE SAME BLOCK!

Bossy
By
Birthright

Bossy By Birthright

SEE THESE COLORING BOOKS? PAY ATTENTION!

I DON'T HAVE TIME TO COLOR EVERY PICTURE MYSELF, UNDERSTAND?

WHAT I WANT YOU TO DO IS GO THROUGH EACH BOOK, AND COLOR ALL THE SKIES BLUE..THEN I WON'T HAVE TO DO IT...

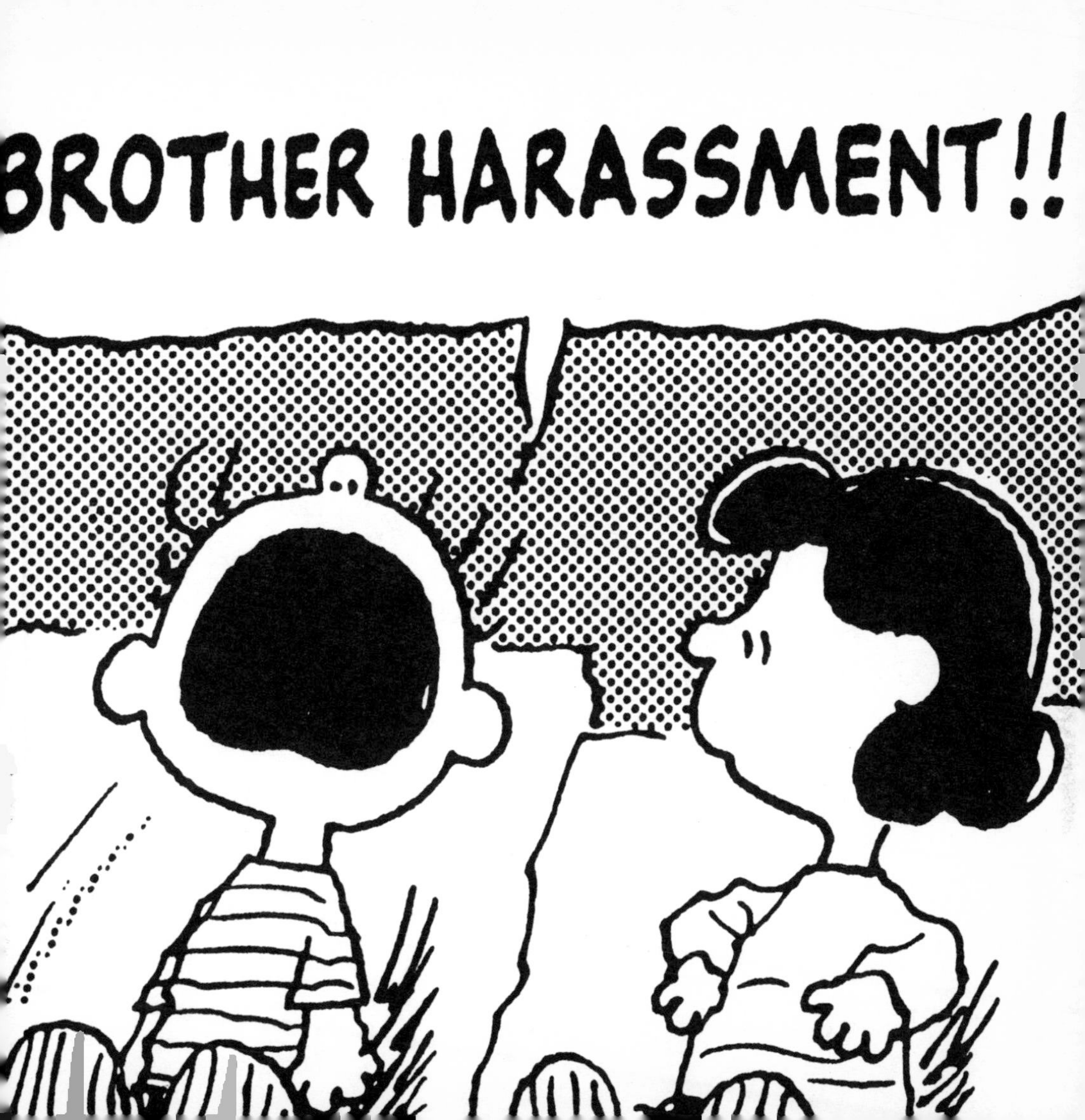
BROTHER HARASSMENT!!

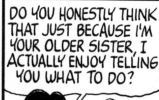

Younger
But
Wiser

 Younger But Wiser

Younger But Wiser

■ HarperCollins*Publishers*

Produced by Jennifer Barry Design, Sausalito, CA.
Creative consultation by 360°, NYC.
First published in 1997 by HarperCollins*Publishers* Inc.
http://www.harpercollins.com

ISBN 0-06-757449-1

Printed in Hong Kong

1 3 5 7 9 10 8 6 4 2

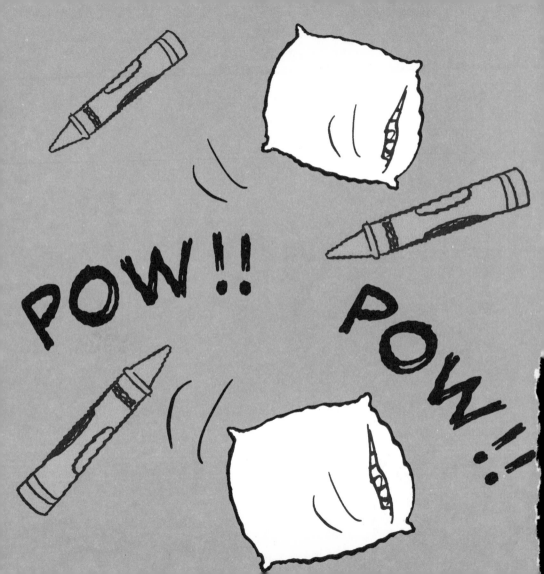